THE MAGIC KITE

Written by Kira Daniel
Illustrated by Marianne Smith Getchell

Troll Associates

Library of Congress Cataloging in Publication Data

Daniel, Kira.
The magic kite.

Summary: Each person in Lauren's class is given a plain white kite and told to make of it the best kite he/she can imagine.
[1. Kites—Fiction] I. Getchell, Marianne Smith, ill. II. Title.
PZ7.D218Mag 1986 [E] 85-14015
ISBN 0-8167-0614-X (lib. bdg.)
ISBN 0-8167-0615-8 (pbk.)

Printed in the United States of America

10 9 8 7 6 5 4 3 2 1

THE MAGIC KITE

It was a breezy Monday morning. Lauren sat at her desk. She looked at her teacher. He was smiling.

"It is March," said Mr. Lee.
"March is a windy month.
March is a great time to fly a
kite."

Lauren loved kites. She liked the way they streamed across the sky on a sunny day.

“We are going to have a kite show,” said Mr. Lee.

Everyone stopped moving.
Everyone was quiet. *What was a kite show?* they wondered.

“What is a kite show?” asked
Lauren.
“Let me explain,” said Mr. Lee.
He took out a bright white
paper kite.

"Today I will give each of you a plain white kite. Change your kite. Make it beautiful. Or funny. Or exciting. Show us your finished kite on Friday. We will see the best kites you can imagine. Then I'll have a surprise for you."

Jon took out his paints. Katie took out bright markers. Dan took out some shiny stickers. He had been saving them for something special. He kept them in his sneaker.

They all started making the most wonderful kites they could imagine. All except Lauren.

She sat with her head in her hands. She closed her eyes. She saw kites covered with tiger stripes. She saw kites made of butterfly wings. She saw kites that flashed liked lightning. How should her kite look? She could not decide.

"I'm lucky it's only Monday," she said.
By Tuesday many kites were finished. Jon held his kite. He looked very happy. He had used every color in his paint box. His kite looked like a rainbow.

"I used about a hundred bows on the tail," he said.
"It's a beautiful kite," said Mr. Lee.
"Nice kite!" said Lauren.
"The tail *really* has only thirty-seven bows," said Katie.

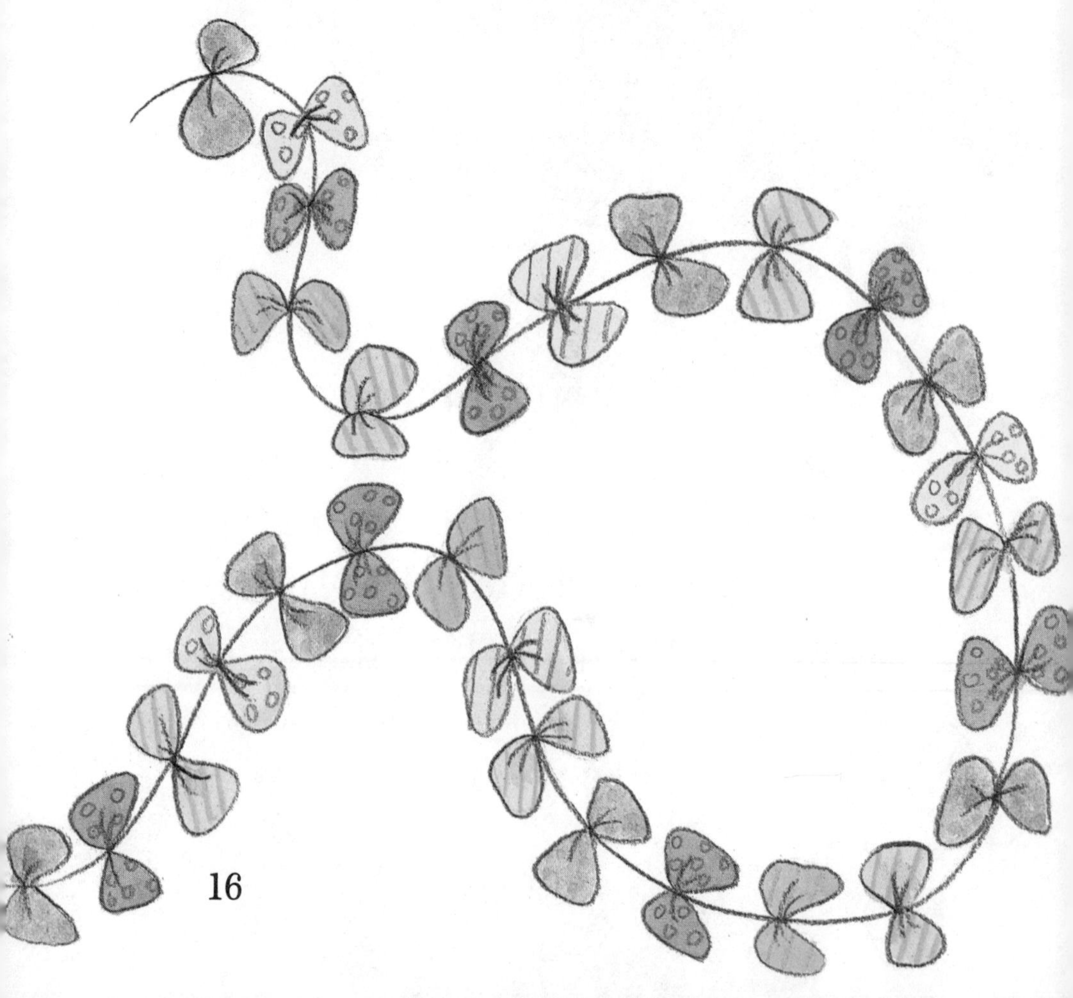

Jon stepped on her toe when
Mr. Lee wasn't looking.

Lauren thought about her kite. It was on her table at home. It was still a plain white kite. She closed her eyes. She saw kites with golden tails flying in the wind. She saw kites that glowed in the dark. She saw kites as light as fluffy clouds. But how should her kite look? She could not decide.

“I’m lucky it’s only Tuesday,”
she said.

On Wednesday Katie showed her kite. It was all finished. Mr. Lee looked at the kite. He laughed.

"What a funny kite, Katie," he said.

Lauren looked at Katie's kite. There was a picture of Katie on it. She was flapping her arms. She was trying to fly. This kite would look funny in the air. Katie would be flying.

“Very silly,” said Jon.
“I think it’s great,” said Lauren.
“It would look better with some stickers,” said Dan.

Lauren's kite had not moved. It was still at her house. It was still on her table. It was still a plain white kite. She thought of kites floating in the sky. Some kites were flying as high as the moon. Some kites had bright faces on them. One kite's tail was two miles long.

“It’s already Wednesday,”
thought Lauren.

On Thursday Dan ran into school with his kite. The kite was covered with shiny stickers. It was a very exciting kite. Everyone agreed.

"My sneakers fit better now, too," said Dan. He showed everyone his empty sneaker.

Lauren was worried.
"Tomorrow is Friday," she thought. "What will I do with my kite?"

That night Lauren looked at her kite. She thought about all her ideas. She imagined a wonderful kite.

It was Friday morning. Everyone held a kite. The room was filled with colors.

"Where is your kite?" asked Katie.

"In my bag," answered Lauren.

"Let's see it," said Jon.

Lauren pulled out her kite. It was plain white.

Someone laughed.

"But there's nothing on it," said Dan. He hugged his own shiny kite.

Someone else laughed. Lauren looked away. She wanted to hide. Then she felt angry.

She said, "I imagined many kites. But this is the best. Sometimes I imagine it is like a summer sunset—all bright pink and blue. Then it changes. It is made of soap bubbles. And I can see through it. It floats up and up. The bubbles pop.

"Then it turns into a bird kite. It has shiny red feathers. It keeps changing and changing. But it always has the same tail. It is a kite with a star-dust tail. The stars reach far across the sky."

"How wonderful," said Mr. Lee. "A kite that changes with your imagination."

No one laughed now. They all looked hard at Lauren's kite.

At first they could see only the plain white kite. Then they began to imagine. Dan saw a kite made of snowflakes. Each snowflake was different. Each twinkled in the sun.

Katie saw flowers—lots of flowers.

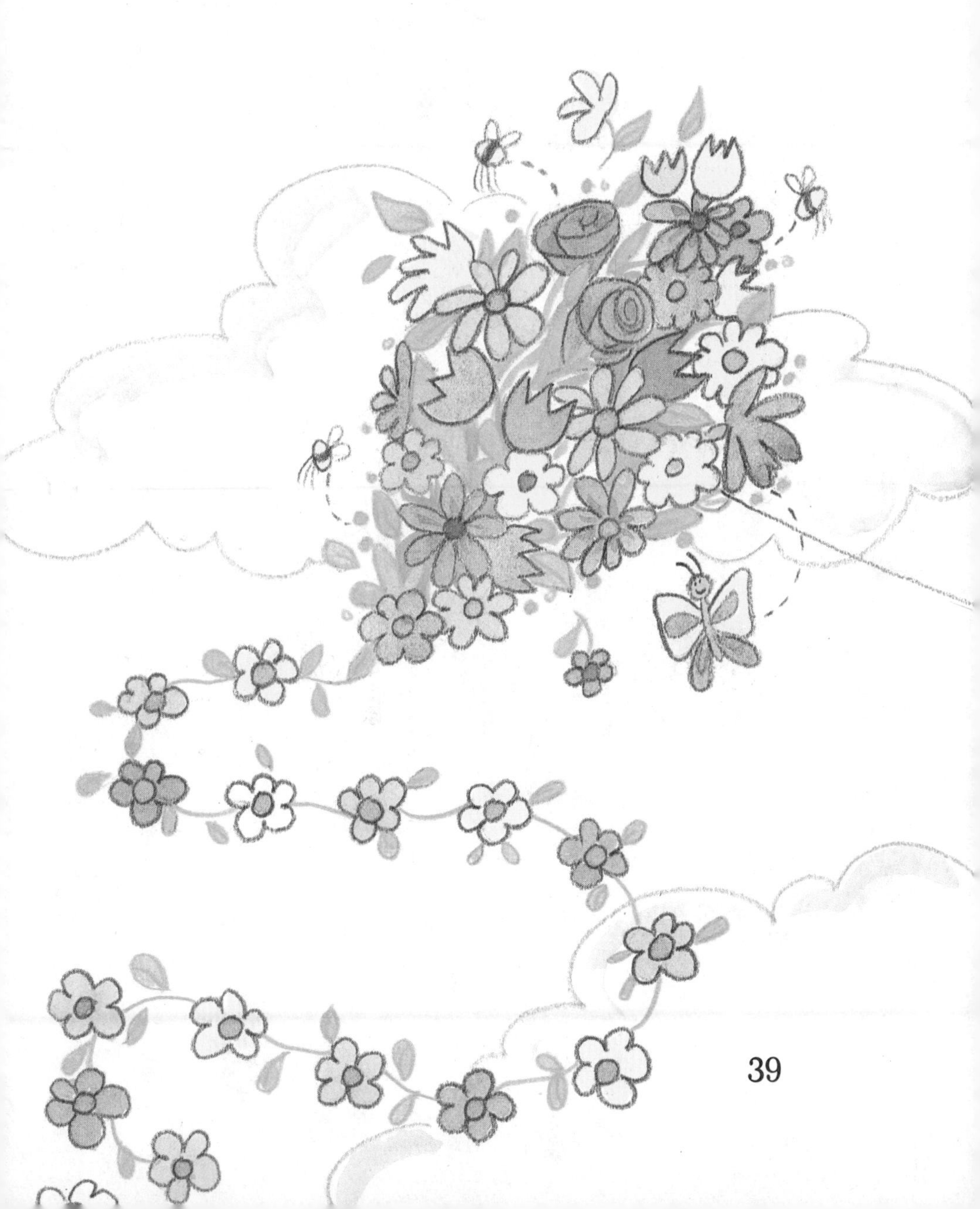

They all saw wonderful things.

"I like your kite," said Dan.

"It's nice," said Katie.

Lauren felt very special.

After the kite show, Mr. Lee said, "Time for my surprise."

Everyone stopped moving.
Everyone was quiet.

"We are going outside to fly the kites," said Mr. Lee. "I will give you each a spool of kite string.

"Watch your kite. See how it looks up in the sky. Think about how it feels to fly."
Everyone went outside. Mr. Lee showed them how to fly the kites.

He ran with them.
He fixed their string.
He cheered with them.